My Li....

Aug 29-08

STORY
BY
MARK MUNNO

Mark Munno (signature)

(signatures)

WRITTEN
BY
TERRI NECCI WIEDMYER

About the author

I am an average person who has had many occupations throughout the years. My most rewarding accomplishment is the creations of the "Peanut" shirt, which was the inspiration for
" My Little Peanut"

"Peanut" artwork copyright
#VAu 742-522

ISBN: 978-0-615-24307-8

ACKNOWLEDGEMENT

I would like to thank Kim Terpstra and
Michele Wingate for all their support in writing
"My Little Peanut"
I would also like to thank my editor Theresa Givvens
for the fine editing of this book and my illustrator Dave
Mantel for the outstanding artwork of this story.
Also my thanks goes out to "Besse Shirt Lettering"
and"Miss Print"printers for all their help in designing
the "Peanut" merchandise.

DEDICATION

I would like to dedicate this book to Virgina Yocco and William Crescent "Crescent Jewelers" Illinois who helped me through some real tough times and for their support and never quit attitude. There are names for people like this they're called angels.

Also, I would like to dedicate this book to my nephew Christopher Stachewicz who suggested the idea for a "Peanut" shirt.

TABLE OF CONTENTS

LIMERICKS

TABLE OF CONTENTS

A Day In The Life Of My Little Peanut

I brush my teeth everyday
To help prevent tooth decay

1.

I tie my shoes so I don't fall
So I can grow to be big and tall
2.

I comb my hair so I look neat
You never know who you will meet

3.

I feed my dog with a smile
Before we go out for a while
4.

My Little Peanut Goes To The Park

One morning My Little Peanut got up early.

Mommy decided to take Little Peanut to the

park to spend the day with Little Peanut's friends.

They all had fun. When the day was over, they

came home. Little Peanut took a short nap.

Mommy made dinner, Daddy came home. They all ate

together. After dinner Mommy, Daddy

and Little Peanut put together a puzzle.

They all had fun spending time together.

It was getting late so Mommy said "it's time

for bed". Little Peanut got tucked in, then

gave Mommy and Daddy a big hug and kiss good night.

My Little Peanut Goes To The Park

My Little Peanut Goes To The Zoo

Mommy and Daddy took My Little Peanut to the zoo.

The first stop was the lion's cage. Little Peanut

never saw a lion. It was a great experience.

The lion nervously paced up and down in the cage,

as everybody walked by.

They saw a tourist train going by. They boarded

the train, it was a great ride. They got to see all the

sights. It was getting dark so they decided to go

home. What a great day!

My Little Peanut Goes To The Zoo

My Little Peanut's Birthday Party

The next day it was My Little Peanut's birthday so

Mommy decided to have a birthday party.

Mommy and Daddy blew up some balloons,

decorated the house and made a

big banner that said "Happy Birthday My Little

Peanut". Everyone started arriving.

After eating they played "Pin The Tail on the

Donkey". Each child was blindfolded and got a paper

tail with a straight pin. The closest one to the

donkey's tail got the prize. Mommy got the cake

ready. Everyone sang "Happy Birthday",

Little Peanut blew out the candles

and everyone got a piece of cake.

It was a very happy day for all.

My Little Peanut's Birthday Party

My Little Peanut Goes To The Museum

It was a beautiful Saturday morning. Mommy and

Daddy decided to take My Little Peanut to the

museum. There were so many great things to see.

Little Peanut was very excited at seeing all the

sights. King Tut's tomb was on the top of the list.

A tour guide took everyone through the tomb.

They saw King Tut's golden chair and his mask.

There were no modern tools, yet everything was

perfect. They also saw a big dinosaur and then

took an elevator down underground to see the

coal mines. The day was very interesting.

My Little Peanut Goes To The Museum

My Little Peanut Helps In The Garden

Mommy said "the first thing we need for our garden is to go shopping for seeds, gloves, hoe, rake and a shovel". The next day Mommy and My Little Peanut went to the garden store and purchased all the gardening supplies.

Mommy said "start digging one inch deep in the ground". They made rows with the hoe and dropped the seeds in the ground one by one.

They covered, patted down and watered the seeds. The tomato plants will need sticks next to them to hold them up when they get to heavy.

My Little Peanut Helps In The Garden

My Little Peanut Is Mommy's Little Helper

My Little Peanut was always curious about cooking.

One day Mommy said "I'll show you how to cook".

First rule is to always have adult supervision

when cooking. Make sure all the pots are

turned away from the stove.

Always wear oven mitts and

have a fire extinguisher handy.

They baked cookies and Mommy let Little Peanut

frost them. Little Peanut was very proud.

It was fun helping Mommy in the kitchen.

THE END

My Little Peanut Is Mommy's Little Helper

"TO BE CONTINUED"

To purchase "Peanut" merchandise
WWW.2MLLC.NET

815—
577-1418